~ No

Dear Abbie,

This is one of our

favorite books —

hope you enjoy it too!

Welcome to PKN!

Kindly. Aki + Kai

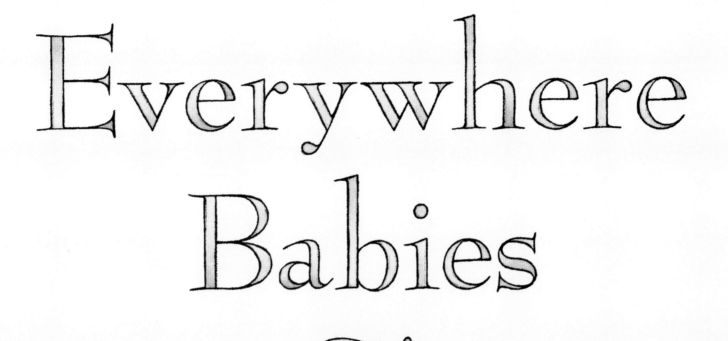

Everywhere Babies

SUSAN MEYERS

ILLUSTRATED BY MARLA FRAZEE

HARCOURT, INC.

San Diego   New York   London

Requests for permission to make copies of any part of the work should be
mailed to the following address: Permissions Department, Harcourt, Inc.,
6277 Sea Harbor Drive, Orlando, Florida 32887-6777.

www.harcourt.com

Library of Congress Cataloging-in-Publication Data
Meyers, Susan.
Everywhere babies/Susan Meyers; illustrated by Marla Frazee.
p. cm.
Summary: Describes babies and the things they do from the time they are
born until their first birthday.
[1. Babies—Fiction. 2. Stories in rhyme.] I. Frazee, Marla, ill. II. Title.
PZ8.3.M5599Ev 2001
[E]—dc21   99-6288
ISBN 0-15-202226-0

C E G H F D

Printed in Singapore

The illustrations in this book were done in pencil and watercolor
on Strathmore paper, hot press finish.
The display type was hand-lettered by Marla Frazee.
The text type was set in Cochin.
Printed and bound by Tien Wah Press, Singapore
Production supervision by Sandra Grebenar and Ginger Boyer
Designed by Kaelin Chappell and Marla Frazee

For Dylan and Trevor,
grandest of babies

—S. M.

With love for Graham, Reed,
and James—every day, everywhere

—M. F.

Every day, everywhere,

fat babies,

thin babies,

small babies,

tall babies,

babies are born~

winter and spring babies,   summer and fall babies.

Every day, everywhere,

on their cheeks,

on their ears,

their fingers,

their nose,

babies are kissed~

on the top of their head,

on their tummy,

their toes.

Every day, everywhere,

in diapers and T-shirts, in buntings and sleepers,

babies are dressed~

in playsuits and dresses, in sweaters and creepers.

Every day, everywhere,

by bottle,
by breast,
with cups,
and with
spoons,

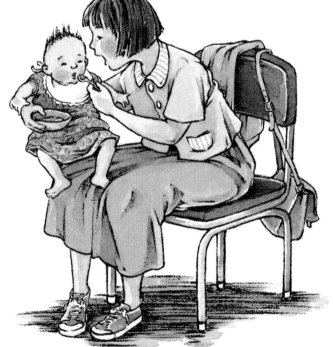

babies are fed~

with milk,
and then
cereal,
carrots,
and
prunes.

Every day, everywhere,

in cradles, in chairs,

at nap time and night,

babies are rocked~

by friends and relations

who cuddle them tight.

Every day, everywhere,

in backpacks,

in front packs,

in slings,

and in strollers,

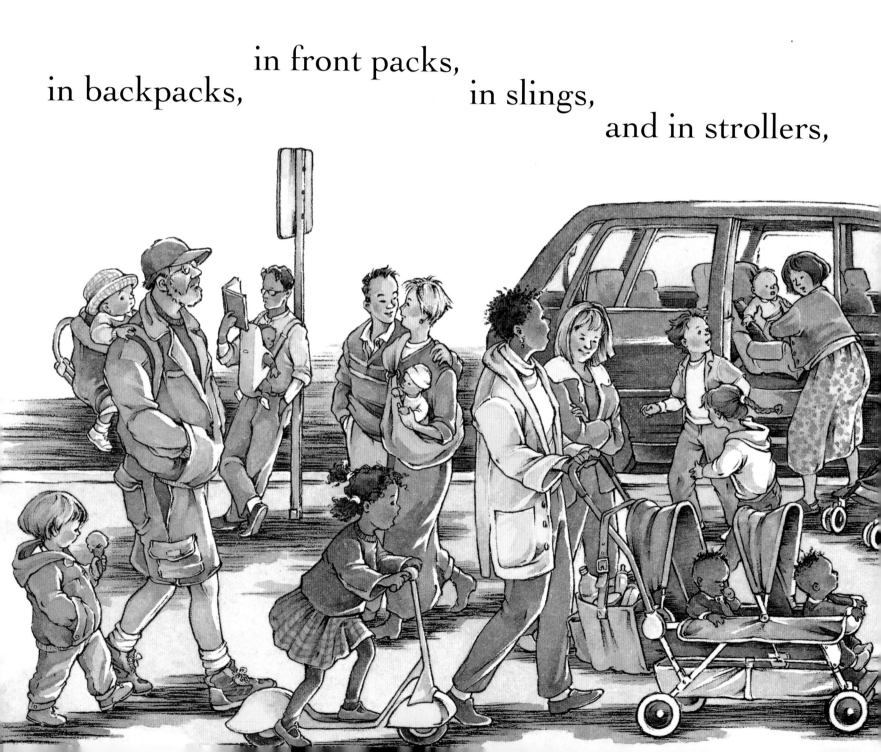

babies are carried~

and bike seats,

in car seats,

and on Daddy's shoulders.

Every day, everywhere,

they cry and they squeal,

they giggle, they coo,

babies make noise~

they clap their hands, too.

they bang and they splash,

Every day, everywhere,

rattles, and tops, and books that won't tear,

babies like toys~

old pots and pans, and a fuzzy brown bear.

Every day, everywhere,

peek-a-boo,

pat-a-cake,

this-little-piggy,

babies play games~

roll-the-ball,

ride-a-horse,

jiggety-jiggy.

Every day, everywhere,

with a puppy,   a kitten,   a goldfish,   a bunny,

babies make friends~

with young people,   old people,   anyone funny.

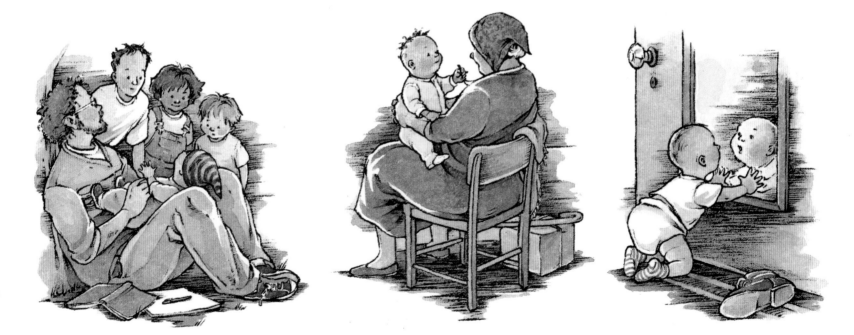

Every day, everywhere,

forward and backward,

on bottoms and knees,

babies are crawling~

wherever they please.

upstairs and downstairs,

Every day, everywhere,

one step, another, they fall down and then . . .

babies are walking~

pick themselves up and try it again.

Every day, everywhere,

they can run,

they can jump,

they can slide,

they can swing,

babies are growing~

they can dig,

they can climb,

they can talk,

they can sing.

Every day, everywhere,

for trying so hard,

for traveling so far,

babies are loved~

for being so wonderful . . .

...just as they are!